MY REAL FAMILY

MY REAL FAMILY

Emily Arnold McCully

BROWNDEER PRESS

HARCOURT BRACE & COMPANY

San Diego   New York   London

For JENNY MACKENZIE LOUGHRIDGE
and her real family

Copyright © 1994 by Emily Arnold McCully

All rights reserved. No part of this publication may be reproduced
or transmitted in any form or by any means, electronic or mechanical,
including photocopy, recording, or any information storage and
retrieval system, without permission in writing from the publisher.

Requests for permission to make copies of any part of
the work should be mailed to: Permissions Department,
Harcourt Brace & Company, 8th Floor, Orlando, Florida 32887.

Library of Congress Cataloging-in-Publication Data
McCully, Emily Arnold.
My real family/by Emily Arnold McCully
p. cm.
"Browndeer Press"
Summary: Sarah, convinced that she is adopted, runs away
from the Bear Family Theater to find her "real parents."
ISBN 0-15-277698-2
[1. Adoption—Fiction.   2. Parent and child—Fiction.
3. Bears—Fiction.   4. Runaways—Fiction.]   I. Title.
PZ7.M478415My   1994
[E]—dc20   92-46290

First edition   A B C D E

Printed in Singapore

The illustrations in this book were done in pen and ink,
watercolor, and pastel on Arches watercolor paper.
The display type was set in Goudy Sans Bold Italic
by Thompson Type, San Diego, California.
The text type was set in Goudy Old Style
by Harcourt Brace & Company Photocomposition Center.
Color separations by Bright Arts, Ltd., Singapore
Printed and bound by Tien Wah Press, Singapore
Production supervision by Warren Wallerstein and Kent MacElwee
Designed by Camilla Filancia

The Strange Pudding was the greatest hit ever presented by the Farm Theater. Sarah's father, Bruno, wrote the play and her mother, Sophie, directed. Her big sister, Zaza, and her brother, Edwin, were the stars. Audiences were delighted. "Zaza was great as the duchess!" they said. "Edwin was a riot as the butler!" What a family! Sarah was very proud. She waited for someone to say something nice about her work on props and costumes.

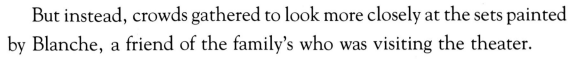

But instead, crowds gathered to look more closely at the sets painted by Blanche, a friend of the family's who was visiting the theater.

"Amazing!" they gasped. "Did a shy little orphan really paint those?" "Blanche is so artistic," they went on. "What a talent that little creature has!"

Sarah began to get sick of hearing it. She couldn't wait for Blanche's grandmother Eva to come and take her home. Sarah wanted her family to herself again.

Finally they put away the costumes and the sets and swept the theater. Then it was time for the celebration. After each production, one of the children got to choose three things: a family activity for the day, what they would eat for dinner, and the bedtime story. It was Sarah's turn, and she had already decided on everything.

"First, let's all go for a hike in the woods," she said.

"Blanche isn't used to the woods," said Sophie.

"She doesn't have to come," said Sarah.

"Sarah!" said Bruno.

"But it's my turn to choose!" cried Sarah.

"I want to watch Blanche sketch and paint," said Zaza.

"That's too boring," said Sarah. "We were all supposed to do some- thing together."

"Be a good sport, Sarah," said Bruno.

Be a good sport? "Hey!" Sarah said. "What about dinner? What about the bedtime story?"

"I thought it might be nice for Blanche to choose the dinner this time," said Sophie.

"I don't *want* to eat Blanche's favorite food," said Sarah.

"Not another word," said Sophie.

It was so unfair! Sarah wished Eva would come right now and take her grandchild away! Everything Sarah had looked forward to was ruined because of Blanche!

After a while, Sophie asked Sarah to set the table.

"Let Blanche set the table!" Sarah said.

"Blanche is busy washing her brushes," said Sophie. "Please put on a better mood, young lady."

How could she do that when her mother and father and sister and brother were behaving like strangers? But she was hungry, so she set the table and sat down.

Before any food appeared, Bruno cleared his throat the way he did when he was about to tell who was getting what part in a play.

"Blanche, dear," he said. "Your grandmother loves you very much, but she is getting too old to take care of a young child. We love having you here. Would you like to stay and live with us?"

"Oh, I would!" said Blanche.

"Since you are an orphan," Bruno went on, "Sophie and I would like to adopt you."

"Hurray!" cried Zaza.

"Yes!" said Edwin.

Sarah was stunned. Her family cared more about Blanche than they did about her.

Sophie said, "Sarah, I think it would be best if you move in with Zaza. Blanche can have your room."

"But I just *got* my own room!" Sarah cried.

"I know," said Sophie. "But Blanche is used to having a quiet place to be alone."

This was the last straw! Sarah shouted "I hate you!" to Sophie and Bruno and ran upstairs.

She threw herself onto her bed—Blanche's bed! Her parents had chosen someone else. She didn't belong to her own family. It might as well be Blanche's family now. In fact . . .

. . . a strange scene appeared in Sarah's mind. Sophie and Bruno were not her real parents. She, Sarah, was adopted!

Somehow she had been separated from her real mother and father. Where were they? Who were they? She wanted to run away into the woods and find them!

If they were in the woods, maybe they were forest rangers! Maybe, after Sarah was born, they had been heroes during a big forest fire and Sarah had gotten lost. Oh, it was so sad! Did she have brothers and sisters? Somehow, she thought not.

Her real parents would be so happy to see her again!

They would all hug and hug and then do things together: build a lean-to out of sticks and branches, lay a campfire, cook some grub. She was still famished!

Sarah decided to find her real parents. It was a little late, but she had to go before it got really dark.

She listened at the back stairs. Voices murmured in the dining room. They were all perfectly happy without her. More proof she was adopted! She grabbed her knapsack and crept down the stairs. To her surprise, she found a pot of ravioli on the stove. It was her favorite dinner—that was strange. Sophie had said they were having Blanche's favorite meal. She dropped a few handfuls in a napkin and put it in her knapsack.

Outside, she plunged into the woods. Her stomach was really growl-
ing now. She popped a ravioli into her mouth. It was OK cold. What
advice would her real parents give her about being in the wild? They
would tell her to leave a trail, just in case she wanted to find her way

back. That was forest ranger procedure, she was sure. The ravioli was all she had, so for each one she ate, she let one fall to the ground.

She walked and walked until she didn't recognize anything. She was deep in the woods now. Her real parents were nowhere in sight.

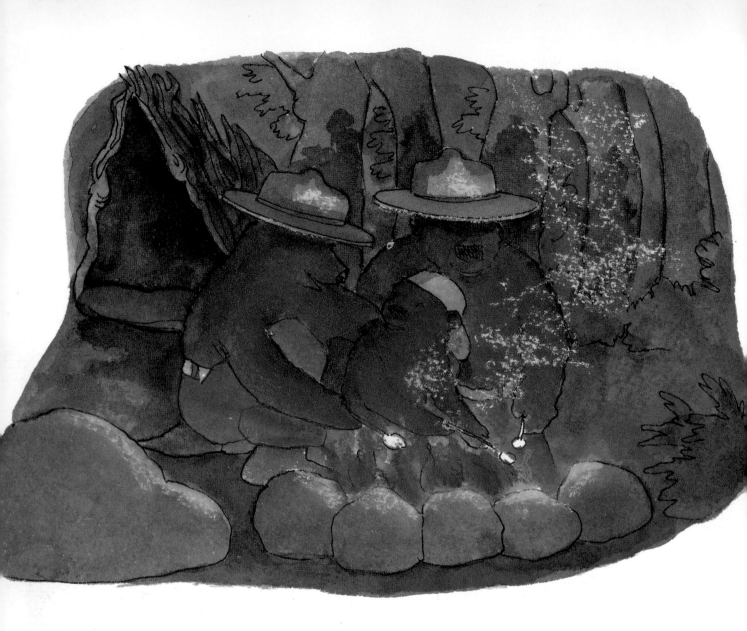

Wherever they were, they must be about to light a campfire. Every night, they cooked their supper and told stories about their lost baby daughter and sang sad songs before the warm, flickering flames. When she found them, Sarah would tell them all about her life at the theater. Her real parents would be amazed to hear about the costumes she had made, the plays she had been in, the audiences' applause.

But there was no sign of a campfire, or anyone.

"Mama? Papa?" she called. The farther she wandered from the Farm Theater, the more she worried that she had made a mistake. If her real parents were forest rangers and they lived right here in these woods, why hadn't they ever come to take her back?

Suppose they didn't live here, and she wasn't going to find them? Sarah sank to the ground, discouraged. It was utterly still in the woods. She could almost see the warm, cozy kitchen at home and almost feel her soft, snugly bed.

Night was falling. She would have to go back to Bruno and Sophie and Zaza and Edwin—and Blanche. They would probably always love Blanche more than they loved her. She would have to get used to that.

Sarah began to trudge back along her trail. First one ravioli, then another, served to guide her. But soon it was pitch-dark and she couldn't see them anymore.

She forged ahead anyway, because it was less scary to keep moving. Then she heard sounds. Voices? She crept ahead and saw a campfire. A family huddled around it, talking together! Sarah's heart leapt. It was just as she had imagined—her own real family, the forest rangers! Did she have brothers and sisters after all?

"I wonder where she is," said the mama. "I hope she's all right!"

"I'm worried sick," said the papa. "If only she would forgive us and come back."

"She's so spunky and smart," said the mama. "She'll turn up!"

"It's all our fault," said one of the children. "We should have gone hiking with her."

"It would have been fun," said another softly.

She was listening to Bruno and Sophie—and everyone else! They had all been looking for her!

"I feel somehow that she is nearby," said Blanche. "I hope she will see the fire."

They wanted her back, even Blanche! Her family loved her after all!

"Here I am!" Sarah cried.

"Sarah!" gasped Sophie.

"My poopsie!" said Bruno. He hadn't called her that since she was about two years old.

"Well, it's about time!" said Zaza gruffly. "We missed you."

"I found these," said Blanche. She was clutching some ravioli.
"They're my favorite."

"Mine too," said Sarah.

"Blanche *knew* you would see our fire!" said Edwin.

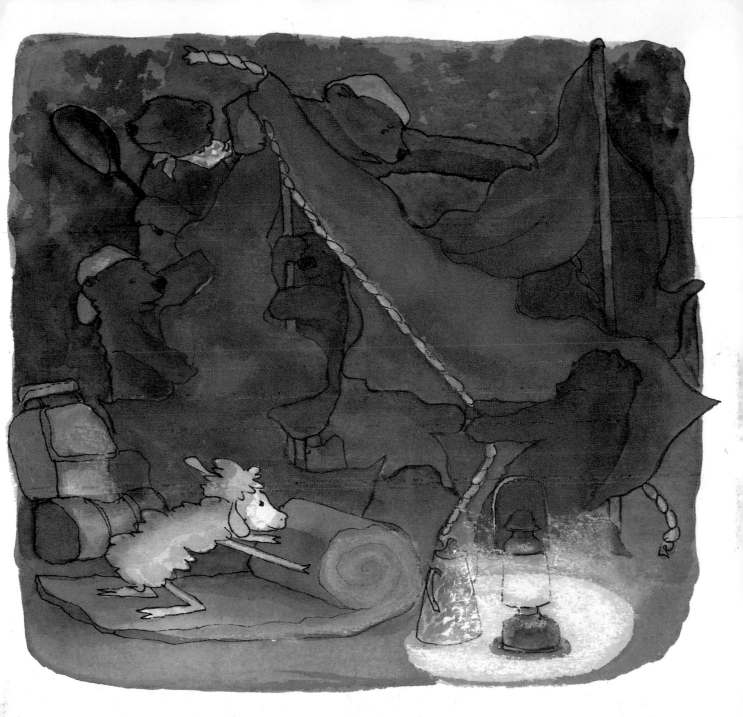

"We'll have to do a lot of camping now that you're back," said Zaza.
"Starting now," said Bruno. "Children, help me put up the tent."
Sarah could see they had enough gear to last for days. "Just in case,"
said Edwin.
"I love you all," said Sarah. "I'm sorry I was grumpy."

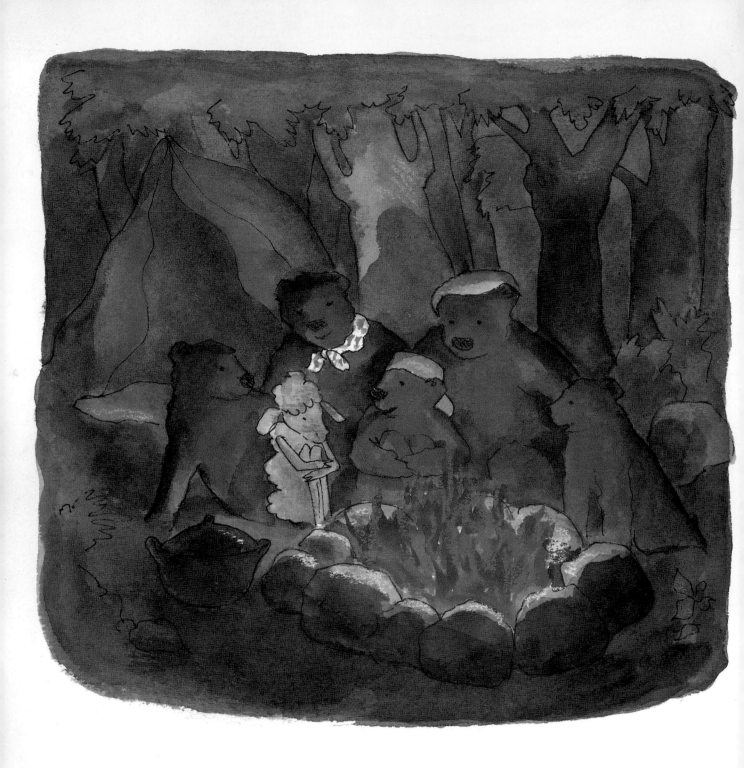

Later, when they were settled around the campfire, Sophie asked, "What bedtime story would you like?"

"The story of a family," said Sarah, "and their found child."